Build It Up

Pan-Canadian Science Place

Pan-Canadian Science Place Team

Gary Cross
Xavier Fazio
Don Kelly
Jo-Anne Lake
Denise MacDonald
Susan Martin
Kathleen Rosborough
Wayne Stewart
Brian Veitch
Barbara Wall
Judy Willson

Scientific Accuracy

Chad Schella
Canadian Construction Association

Scholastic Canada Ltd.

Build It Up

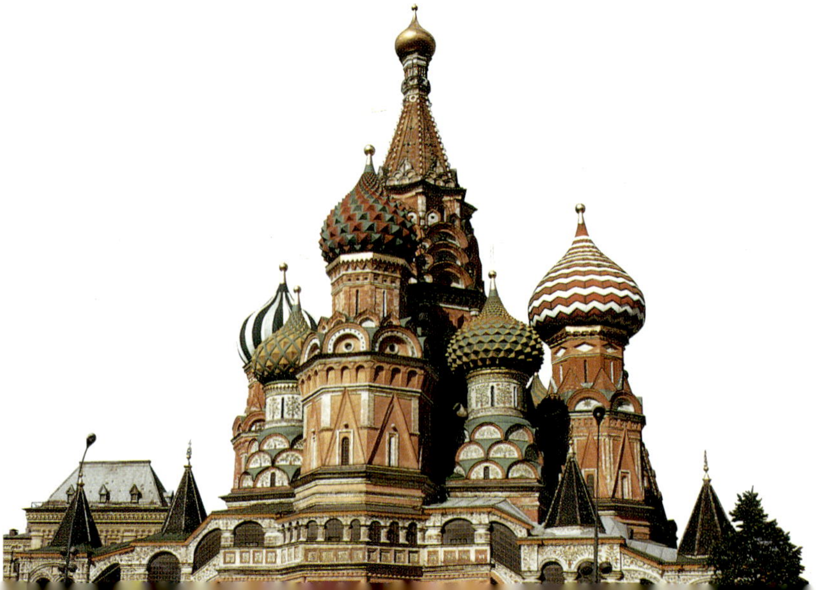

This symbol tells you when to write in your Science Journal.

This symbol shows you when to be careful.

Words in **green** are explained in the glossary on page 32.

What Are Structures?

All over the world, people build different kinds of structures for different purposes. Structures have many parts. Houses, bridges, tents, ladders, and tables are all structures. What are these structures used for?

Animals and plants build structures, too. What natural structures can you think of?

Look for structures.

You need:
- pencil
- paper
- crayons or markers

1 Make a chart to compare structures in your community. You could compare the purpose, size, and shape of structures. What else could you compare?

2 Choose a part of your community to examine. Draw pictures and write about the different structures you see there.

3 What structures did you see? What are they used for? Use your pictures and notes to fill in your chart.

People build different kinds of structures than plants and animals. How are they different? How are they the same?

People called architects design each structure according to how it will be used. They plan the structure's shape and decide what materials it will be made of.

LESSON 2

What Are the Parts of a Building?

Buildings are places where people live, work, or store things. Schools, apartments, and fire stations are buildings. What other buildings can you think of?

Buildings have different uses, but they have many of the same parts. All buildings have doors, windows, walls, floors, and a roof. What other parts do all buildings have? How many different parts and materials can you observe in a building?

Become building-parts experts.

You need:
- pencil
- paper
- crayons or markers

1. Have each member of your group choose a different building part. Look for your part in four different buildings, including your school. How is this part shaped in each building? What materials is it made of? How else could you find out about your building part?

2. In words and pictures, make a report about your building part. Share the report with your group and your class.

How do the parts of these buildings tell you what the buildings are used for?

Many of the materials used in structures are prepared before construction begins. Some of these materials are lumber, bricks, shingles, and glass. Some building parts, such as windows and doors, are also made before construction begins. All building materials and parts have to be measured carefully. Why would that step be important?

How Does a Foundation Work?

Most structures are made of heavy materials. The bottom part, the foundation, has to support all the mass. It needs to hold the structure straight up. The foundation cannot move; it must be stable. Why do you think this is important? What does a stable foundation look like?

Be a foundation.

1. Find a partner. Choose one person to be the foundation and the other person to be the wind.

2. **Foundation:** Stand up straight with your legs together.
Wind: Give the foundation a gentle push from the side. Does the foundation tip over easily? (The foundation tips over when it moves at least one leg.)

3. **Foundation:** Stand up straight but spread your feet apart.
Wind: Give the foundation another gentle push. How easily does the foundation tip over now?

4. Switch roles with your partner and repeat steps 2 and 3.

5. How could you move your body to make it more stable? Test your ideas with your partner.

What are foundations made of? When water and sand are mixed with cement, they make concrete. Builders often pour concrete for foundations. It hardens into a very strong material.

Other foundations are made of stones or concrete blocks cemented together. Where would you look to find out what kind of foundation your school or home has?

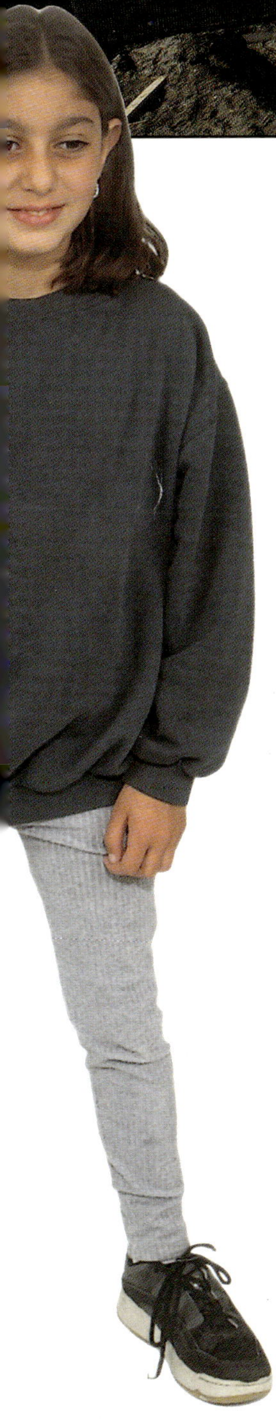

▼ Why do you think the Leaning Tower of Pisa, in Italy, leans? How could it be fixed?

What Materials Make Strong Building Frames?

Every structure has a frame. The frame holds the structure together the way the bones in your body hold together your muscles and skin. The frame supports the other parts of the structure.

In building frames, the wood or metal pieces that stand up are called posts. The pieces that lie sideways are called beams. The more floors a building has and the heavier its roof is, the stronger the frame has to be. What materials make strong frames?

Test posts and beams.

You need:
- 4 craft sticks
- 8 straws
- scissors
- modelling clay
- marbles
- milk-carton bottom
- string

❶ Cut four of your straws as long as the sticks. Predict which will make stronger posts and stronger beams: the sticks, the short straws, or the long straws.

❷ Use pieces of modelling clay to hold up four sticks in the shape of a square. Put the milk-carton bottom on top of the posts, like a floor, and add marbles. How many marbles can the sticks hold?

❸ Now test the sticks as beams. Hold one sideways and hang the milk-carton bottom from it. How many marbles can the stick hold? Is the wood stronger when you use it flat or on its edge?

❹ Repeat steps 2 and 3 using short and long straws. How is each material strongest? How strong a frame could you make using posts and beams?

What Shapes Make Strong Building Frames?

The frame of a structure needs strong materials because it holds the structure together. The way the materials are shaped and put together can also help the frame support weight. You have seen how posts and beams work in square shapes. Now think about arches, or curves, and triangles. Which do you think are the stronger shapes—arches, triangles, or squares?

Carry the weight.

1. Place an index card between two pieces of modelling clay to make a gently curved arch. Fold another card in thirds to make a square post-and-beam shape. Stand it between two pieces of modelling clay.

2. Which shape do you think will support more weight, the arch or the square?

3. Place the milk-carton bottom or yogurt cup on top of each shape and add marbles to it. How many marbles does each shape hold?

4. Fold an index card into a triangle so that it fits under the post-and-beam shape. Tape its loose edges together and slide it under the post and beam. Now how many marbles can the beam hold?

◄ A hydro tower

▲ The Colosseum in Rome was built of brick, concrete, and stone and was completed in the year 80 AD.

Arches and triangles are strong because some of the weight resting on them pushes sideways instead of down. How did your post-and-beam shape change under all the weight?

Look at the structures in these pictures and in your classroom. Where do you see arches? Where do you see triangles? How could you use triangle and arch shapes to strengthen the posts and beams you made in the last exploration?

THINK!
How are you working like a strong shape when you sit back to back with a friend?

How Can You Make the Shapes in Structures Stronger?

Triangles are strong shapes. They are also rigid. That means the sides do not bend easily. Which parts of a structure need to be rigid? How can you make different shapes more rigid?

Make shapes stronger.

You need:
- pipe cleaners

1 Use pipe cleaners to make a square, a rectangle, and a pentagon (a five-sided shape). Make sure the sides of each shape are the same length.

2 Lay each shape on your desk and pull gently on opposite corners. Now press the opposite corners together. What happens to each shape when you pull or push?

3 How can you strengthen each shape? Add pieces of pipe cleaner to your shapes to make them stronger. How many pieces did you have to add?

Be Aware! Be careful if you use scissors to cut pipe cleaners.

Builders often add pieces to the frame of a structure to strengthen it. The extra pieces keep other parts of the frame from moving in or out, just the way your pipe cleaners did.

▲ **The Lethbridge Viaduct**

The shapes in a structure are often divided into triangles. Look at the pictures on this page. Where do you see triangles? What other shapes do you see?

THINK!
What do you think would happen to a triangle if you took away the beam along the bottom?

▼ **A truss bridge is made of many triangles.**

How Is a Dome Used in Buildings?

Another shape used in structures is the dome. Domes can be used for roofs or for whole buildings. A dome is like an upside-down bowl. Arches curve in one direction; what directions do domes curve in? How strong do you think domes are?

Make a dome home.

You need:
- pipe cleaners
- modelling clay
- milk-carton bottom
- marbles

1. Make four arches out of four pipe cleaners. Use pieces of modelling clay to hold the ends to the table, and stand them together to make a frame for a dome.

2. With another four pipe cleaners, make a square structure. Hold it down with pieces of modelling clay.

3. Use the milk-carton bottom to hold the marbles and test the strength of each structure. Which shape is stronger?

4. Try to rebuild the weaker shape to make it as strong as the other one. Now which shape has more space inside it?

Domes need less material to give the same amount of inside space as a building with straight sides. Domes do not need inside walls to help support the roof. How could these things be good?

Dome roofs cover observatories, cathedrals, and stadiums. What other structures are dome shaped?

▲ **This is the SkyDome in Toronto, Ontario.**

► **St. Basil's Cathedral in Moscow, Russia, has onion domes.**

What Materials Make Good Roofs?

The frame and the walls of a building are usually covered by a roof. Some bridges are also covered by a roof. What does a roof do for a structure? Think about different kinds of hats people wear. What do hats do?

Most materials inside a structure are not waterproof, so a rainstorm can mean big trouble. How could a roof help prevent that kind of trouble?

You need:
- cloth
- aluminum foil
- tarpaper
- scissors
- craft sticks
- tape
- a pan
- milk-carton sides
- a sponge
- a cup of water
- sand

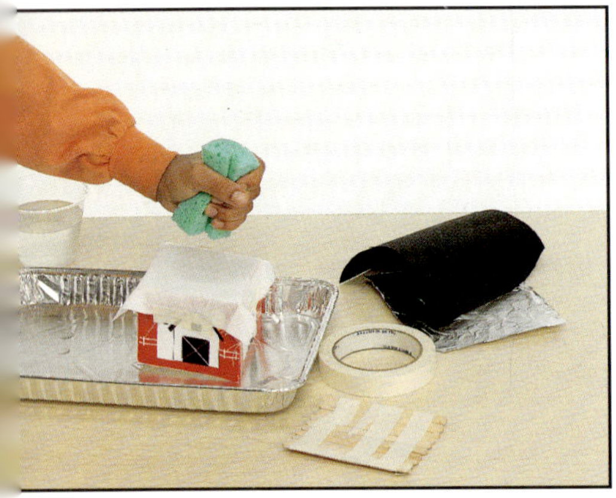

Find a good roof.

1. Use the milk-carton sides for walls. Cut the cloth, foil, and tarpaper into pieces that will cover your walls like a roof. Tape some wood sticks together to make another roof covering.

2. Think of ways to test each of the materials for rain, wind, and other kinds of weather. Tape each material to the top of your walls and test it. Carefully observe what happens each time. What else could happen to a roof?

3. Try to combine materials to make better roofs. Which materials and combinations work best?

► **Roofs can be made of plastic or rubber.**

A metal roof

Some roofing materials, like tarpaper, come in big rolls. Metal roofing comes in long strips. Shingles are usually small pieces. Some roofs are made of two or three materials combined. No matter what materials are used, all the pieces are put down with overlapping edges. How could that make a better roof?

▼ **A roof made of straw is a thatched roof.**

THINK!
How could you use leaves to make a roof?

How Are Building Materials Joined Together?

Joints are places where two or more pieces of a structure are joined together. How did you join the pipe cleaners in Lesson 7? How have you joined materials in other lessons?

Sometimes you can make a joint without extra materials. Sometimes you need to use another material, like tape or modelling clay. How many different joints can you make?

▲ **Gussets are pieces of material that make joints stronger. Gussets are often made of metal. You can make gussets using cardboard or construction paper. ▼**

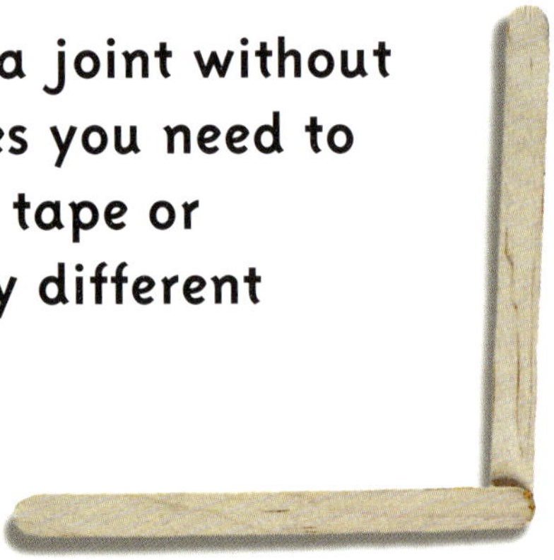

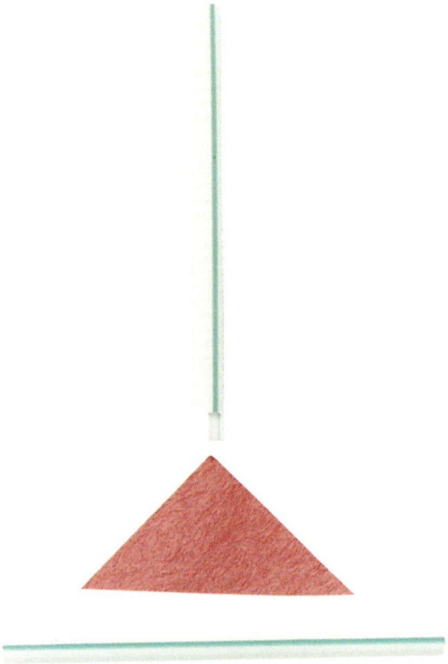

Join together.

1. Make a list of the building materials and joining materials in your class.

2. Pick one building material and make a square post-and-beam shape. How will you join your posts and beams?

3. Use modelling clay to hold your post-and-beam shape up on the table. Push down on the posts. How strong are your joints? Do they move?

4. Find another way to join your posts and beams. Test the new joints. How many joints can you think of? Which joints are strongest? Which joints move?

THINK!
Where are the joints in your body?

◄ **A hinge joins a door to the wall. The hinge lets the door open and close. Where else can you find hinges? How can you make a hinge using your materials?**

How Can You Build a Skyscraper?

What does a skyscraper feel like? Skyscrapers are the world's tallest buildings. The frame of a skyscraper has to support the floors, walls, windows, and roof. It must also hold up the people and furniture inside.

You need:
- old newspapers
- masking tape

Build a skyscraper.

1. Make a drawing of how you want your skyscraper to look.

2. Roll each page of newspaper and tape it. Bend and join the rolls to make the foundation and frame of your skyscraper. You can use tape to join two or more rolls together.

3. Add more newspaper rolls to your frame. How can you use triangles and arches to strengthen it? How else can you strengthen your frame? How can you change your foundation to build a taller skyscraper?

Be Aware! Don't climb on furniture if your skyscraper gets very tall.

▲ **Before 1885, tall buildings had six storeys. Now they are as high as 110 storeys. These skyscrapers are in Vancouver.**

▲ **Steel beams in the shape of an I are very strong and not as heavy as solid square beams.**

► **Steel bars make concrete stronger.**

A tall building would need such thick foundations of stone or brick that other buildings could not stand near it. What kinds of foundations do you think skyscrapers need?

When people invented steel I-beams, new buildings could be taller and heavier. Can you think of another invention that let skyscrapers reach for the sky?

What Tools Do Builders Use?

Builders use tools to measure, cut, push, pull, and join materials. What do the tools on this page do? What tools have you used to build?

Large machines help builders do big jobs. They can dig holes for foundations, push soil and rocks out of the way, and move beams and posts.

Tools and machines can be dangerous. Builders use them properly and carefully. They wear special clothing and equipment to protect themselves. How could the tools on these pages hurt someone? How could the tools in your classroom hurt someone?

▲ On a construction site, special signs warn people of danger. Sometimes, these signs tell builders to wear special equipment. What do you think this sign means?

LESSON 12

What Can You Do With a Lever?

Many building tools are levers. A lever helps you move things easily or quickly. A seesaw, a crowbar, and a hammer are all levers.

▲ You can lift a friend high up in the air with a seesaw.

▲ You can move a rock with a crowbar.

◀ You can pull a nail out of a board with a hammer.

See how levers work.

1. Pick one of the levers and look at it. What is it? Who uses it?

2. Use your lever. What does your lever do? Can you do the same thing without using your lever?

3. Which parts of your lever move when you use it? What do you do when you use your lever? Do you push, pull, or lift?

4. Explain your lever to the class. How are the different levers the same? How are they different?

Be Aware!

Don't get your fingers caught in the lever.

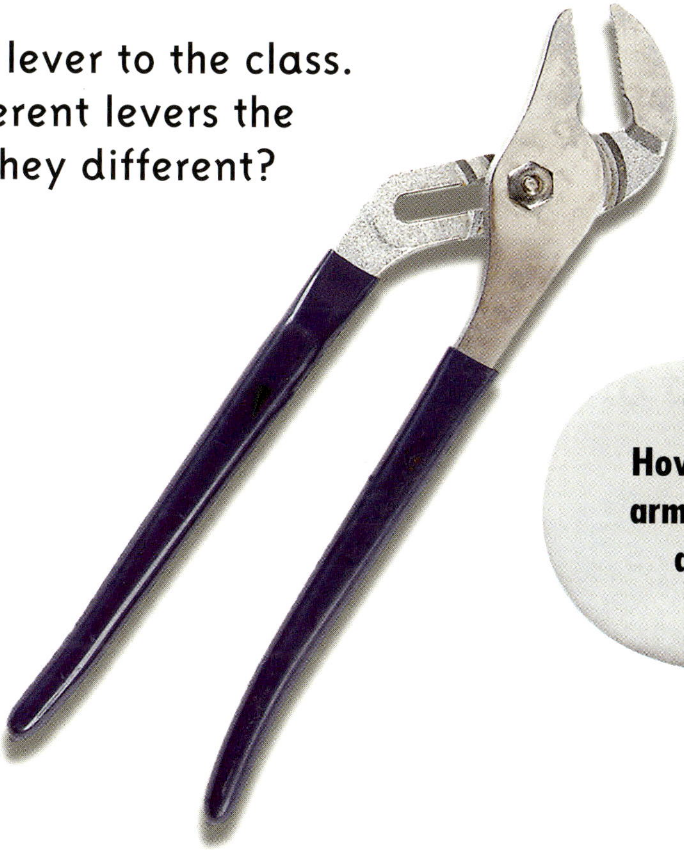

How Can You Build a Bridge?

People build bridges to cross rivers, lakes, and valleys. People cross bridges in cars, in trains, and on bicycles. What other reasons can you think of for building a bridge?

Bridges can be made of many different materials, like steel, wood, or concrete. All bridges must be strong enough to support the mass of the people and vehicles that will cross them. How can you build a strong bridge?

Build a bridge.

1 Place the two piles of books 30 cm apart. This is the distance your bridge must cross. Your bridge must also support the mass of at least two toy cars.

2 Think about how your bridge will look. What shapes and materials will you use? How will you make your shapes and materials strong? How will you join your materials?

3 Draw pictures of what your bridge will look like.

4 Build your bridge. Test your bridge using the milk-carton bottom and marbles. Does your bridge move or bend? Do you need to make your bridge stronger? Pick one thing you would like to change about your bridge and do it.

5 Look at the bridges your classmates have made. What did the strongest bridge look like? What was it made of?

You need:
- 2 toy cars
- 2 piles of books
- student building materials
- marbles
- milk-carton bottom

THINK!
How would you have to change your bridge if it had to cross a very wide river or valley?

How Do People Design Structures?

Structures are like puzzles. All the pieces must be put together just right for the building to work as people planned. The experts who design and construct a structure work together as a team to answer questions like these: What is the purpose of the structure? Where will it be located? How can we make it safe for the people who will use it? How will it look?

Design a playground.

You need:
- pencil
- paper
- crayons or markers

❶ Visit a playground in your community and look at pictures of playgrounds. What kinds of structures are in a playground? What do they look like? What is your favourite playground structure? As a group, decide what makes a good playground.

❷ Decide what structures will be in your playground. What will their purpose be? How big will they be? What else do you need to decide before you try to design your playground?

❸ Draw some pictures of your playground and pick the one that you think will work best.

❹ Present your design to the class. What do people think of your design? Do they have any suggestions to make it safer or better for the people who will use it?

THINK!
What jobs do you think there are on a building team and which would you like to do?

arch
[arch]

An arch is a curved structure. The separate parts of the curve all push against one another and hold up the arch.

architect
[AR-kuh-TEKT]

An architect designs structures. To do so, the architect thinks about the purpose of the structures, the weather they will exist in, and the money and materials available for them.

beam
[beem]

A beam is a long piece lying sideways in a building frame. It is usually made of wood or metal and works with posts and other beams to support a structure.

building
[BIL-ding]

A building is a structure built for people to use. Schools, apartments, hotels, fire stations, and libraries are buildings.

concrete
[KON-kreet]

Concrete is a mixture of sand, gravel, cement, and water. It starts as a thick liquid but it becomes very hard. Steel bars in the liquid make concrete even stronger.

dome
[dome]

A dome is a circular structure in which the sides and top curve together. Roofs and whole buildings can be shaped like domes.

engineer
[EN-juh-NEER]

Engineers plan and build structures. They figure out the exact sizes and kinds of materials that will make a building safe for its purpose and location.

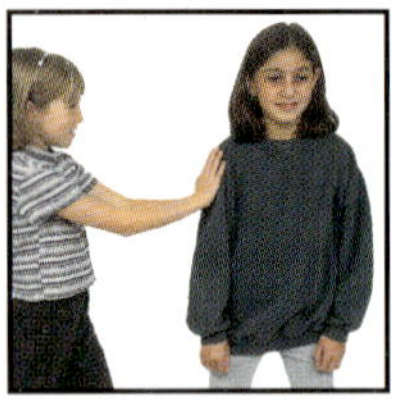

foundation
[fown-DAY-shun]

A foundation is the base that supports a building and holds it firmly to the ground. The bigger the building, the stronger its foundation needs to be.